GETTYSBURG

Me and Pa

Tad Lincoln

GETTYSBURG

Tad Lincoln's Story

F. N. MONJO

illustrations by Douglas Gorsline

Windmill Books Inc.
and E. P. Dutton & Co. Inc.
New York

J
Monjo

Text copyright © 1976 by F. N. Monjo
Illustrations copyright © 1976 by Douglas Gorsline
All rights reserved
Published by Windmill Books & E. P. Dutton & Co., Inc.
201 Park Avenue South, New York, New York 10003

Library of Congress Cataloging in Publication Data

Monjo, F. N. Gettysburg.

Bibliography:

Summary: Recounts the events of the Battle of Gettysburg
and the dedication of the cemetery there,
as seen through the eyes of Tad Lincoln.

1. Gettysburg, Battle of, 1863—Juvenile fiction.
[1. Gettysburg, Battle of, 1863—Fiction.
2. Lincoln, Abraham, Pres. U.S. 1809-1865—Fiction.
3. Lincoln, Thomas, 1853-1871—Fiction]
I. Gorsline, Douglas W. II. Title.

PZ7.M75Ge   [Fic]   75-6695   ISBN 0-525-61534-2

Published simultaneously in Canada by Clarke, Irwin & Company, Limited,
Toronto and Vancouver

Printed in the U.S.A.   First Edition
10 9 8 7 6 5 4 3 2 1

GETTYSBURG

a young soldier

Tad Lincoln

My real name is Thomas, but Pa calls me Tad. That's because he thought I looked like a tadpole, when I was a baby, seeing I had such a big head and such a skinny little body. Now everybody calls me Tad.

Pa has to work hard being President, because we're in the middle of this terrible war. Pa calls it "the rebellion." There's thirteen Southern states fighting against the Union, and they've been at it way over two years, now. At first, we had nothing much but defeats. Then, this past July, we had some victories. And I asked Pa a lot of questions about the biggest one of all—the one at Gettysburg. He explained it to me, like I thought he would.

During the time Pa was sick—last November, in 1863— we couldn't go into his room. So he sent me a message telling me that he'd do something nice with me, just as soon as he got well. You know what he had? Smallpox. Just a light case. He joked about it.

People are always asking Pa for favors. That's because he's President, and they think he's got lots of jobs to hand out to anybody who asks.

When he caught smallpox, right after he got back from his trip to Gettysburg, Mama told me he smiled and said, "Now I've got something I can give to *everybody*."

Soon as he got better from the smallpox, around last Thanksgiving, Pa asked me what I wanted that "something nice" to be—that something he'd promised me he'd do when he was well. I told him I wanted him to take me down to the Navy Yard to see all those big, burly Russian sailors from the Russian navy. They've sailed over here on their fleet, on a good-will tour. Pa says they're going to spend the winter here. And he was real happy about it, because that will show the rest of the world that the Czar of Russia is our friend.

We need friends real bad, now, with the war on. There's two powerful foreign countries who wouldn't be so sorry to see us lose. You know who they are? France and England. They almost came right out and helped the Rebels fight against us. But Pa says now that we've won the battle of Gettysburg, he don't think they'll dare to think about offering any help to the South anymore. Not now that it looks like we Yankees are bound to win.

Gettysburg was a terrible big three-day battle. Pa showed me all about it on the maps he's got on the wall of his office in the White House. He always has pins stuck in them maps, showing where the armies are. Red pins for the Rebs. And blue for the Union.

Every night, pretty near, Pa walks over to the War Department. So he can talk to Mr. Stanton, his Secretary of War, and to General Halleck, his General in Chief. That's where Pa reads all the telegrams coming into the telegraph office, telling how our Union armies are making out, all over the country, wherever they're fighting.

Sometimes Pa takes me along, too. Then the boys in the

Edwin M. Stanton

Gen. Henry W. Halleck

telegraph office say, "Good evening, Mr. Lincoln. Good evening, Tad." Then Pa takes off that gray plaid shawl he always wears, and throws it over the top of the screen door that opens into Mr. Stanton's office, and sits down. Sometimes, when things are going real bad for our side, he'll stay there all night long, reading telegrams, and sending messages to generals, telling them to fret the enemy and to push him, and to take him by the throat, like a bulldog, and chew and chew. Real sharp messages, like that! Pa's dead serious about winning this war.

Sometimes he tells jokes to the boys in the office, rubbing his long legs with his big hands the way he does. But mostly he just sits there arguing with General Halleck and Mr. Stanton, and reading telegrams.

It takes a long time to read those telegrams coming in. Because they write all of them in cipher. Now, cipher is a kind of secret code, and they use it so that if the Rebels are able to get hold of a telegraph message, by mistake, they won't be able to read it.

Here's the way it works. Suppose the telegram says "Asia." Well, that stands for General Grant. Suppose it says "Cambria." That's Washington, D.C. In cipher, you say "Embrace" when you really mean Virginia. You say "Chester" when you mean Attacked. General Meade is "Abel." And guess who "Andes" is? That's Abraham Lincoln, my Pa!

I know both the cipher names for Jefferson Davis, the Rebels' president, and for their best general, General Robert E. Lee—they each got *two* cipher names. Jeff Davis is "Hosannah" or "Husband." General Lee is "Hunter" or "Happy."

Me and Pa and Mr. Stanton at the War Department

So, if a telegram coming in says

HAPPY CHESTER ABEL

you can figure out from the cipher books that it's really saying

LEE ATTACKED MEADE . . .

which is just exactly what happened up at Gettysburg, back in July.

Well, "Happy" and "Hosannah" may be what the cipher books call those two Rebel leaders. But that's not what *Pa* calls them. He calls them "Bobby Lee and Jeffie D." Same as if they was two bad little boys. It upsets him something awful when they talk about "our beloved country." Because they don't mean the United States when they say that. They're talking about the Confederacy, same as if it was a country all to itself. Pa gets mighty angry when he reads that stuff in their newspapers. He says it's all a pack of nonsense and humbug. And he isn't going to let them wreck our Union and pull this country in two, no matter *what* they think. "Our beloved country," my eye! Pa says every square inch of their "beloved country" is still part of the United States of America, and it's going to *stay* that way.

I told Pa I figured he must hate the Rebels a whole lot, for trying to bust this country apart. But Pa sure surprised me. He told me he really didn't hate 'em. It wasn't as simple as all that, he said. Because, he told me, he thought *he* might have turned out to be a Rebel himself, if he'd happened to be living down there in the South.

It made me think a lot different about this war, when Pa

Gen. Robert E. Lee

said that. Made it harder to understand, too. But it showed me that beating the South wasn't the big thing. Having our country back, whole, in one piece, is all that matters.

But Bobby Lee and Jeffie D. sure didn't see things that way. They was sure they could win. They'd already defeated General McClellan at Antietam. They'd whipped General Burnside at Fredericksburg. And they beat General Hooker at Chancellorsville.

So, around about early last June, Bobby Lee decided he was going to leave our Union general, old "Fighting Joe" Hooker, and his Army of the Potomac, right there, in Virginia, while Lee would scoot up the Shenandoah Valley, get the cannons and soldiers and wagons of his Army of Northern Virginia across the Potomac River, and plunge into Maryland and Pennsylvania. That way, Lee could pick up lots of food and horses and ammunition and supplies from all the farms and towns in Pennsylvania. His army didn't have half enough of anything of that kind.

Pa told me some people were saying that Lee might try to capture Washington, or Baltimore, or Harrisburg. Maybe even Philadelphia or New York! They said he might wreck all the railroads, and set all the coal mines on fire, up there in Pennsylvania. That would leave all our navy steamships and our locomotives with no coal to burn!

Folks was in a panic when they realized his army was on the move. Post offices and schools shut down. Railroad trains quit running. Bankers in all those little towns out in western Pennsylvania packed up all their money and sent it to Philadelphia for safekeeping.

People began building barricades in the streets of Baltimore, and in lots of other towns. Farmers tried to hide their food and horses, because they knew the Rebels would grab anything they could get their hands on. General Lee was offering to *pay* for whatever he took, of course. Trouble was, he only aimed to pay in Confederate money—and everybody knew *that* wasn't going to be worth a plugged nickel if the South lost the war.

Worst off of all was the poor Black folks. Plenty of them, living up there in Pennsylvania, were free men. And some others had run away, long ago, from slavery in the South. But if any of them got caught by Lee's army, they'd get took prisoner, and be shipped back down to Virginia—where they'd be sure to end up slaves.

No wonder they was in a worse panic, even, than all the white folks. Some of them was hid in attics and cellars by their white friends. Others put all their stuff in wagons, and started heading north, trying to escape the Rebel army.

Pa's red pins kept crawling up his map as Lee's men pushed further and further into Pennsylvania. Bobby Lee scattered his army all over the western half of the state. Some of it was in Chambersburg. Some raided Gettysburg for supplies and went on to plunder York. Another big part of his soldiers captured Carlisle and drove on over to the Susquehanna River, ready to take Harrisburg, the state capital, on the opposite bank.

Sometimes the Rebels would threaten to burn down a town unless the people there would give them all the money, or the flour, or the horses, or the shoes they was asking for. Usually the towns didn't have half enough of what Bobby Lee's men was demanding.

Of course, there were some people—mostly in Maryland —glad to see the Rebels, because they was hoping the South would win.

I wondered what it would be like if *I* was a Southern boy, and my Ma and Pa was for Bobby Lee and Jeffie D. I guess I would have felt glad to see that big gray army come tramping up those winding roads, their uniforms all covered with white dust, their columns twisting and turning like a long ribbon, through those cornfields and wheatfields lying there ripening under the hot June sun. Their bands would be playing songs like *Dixie*, and *The Bonnie Blue Flag*, and *Maryland, My Maryland*. I reckon I'd of been proud of Robert E. Lee—hoping he'd ask me if I'd like to ride up beside him, for a spell, on his big gray horse, Traveller. Might even have picked him a basket of ripe raspberries, just to be friendly.

But of course I *ain't* a Southern boy. I'm Tad Lincoln, true blue, through and through. I'm for the Union, and I've got me a colonel's uniform in the Army of the Potomac. And Pa got General Halleck to write me out my commission, same as any other officer. So why do you suppose these thoughts ever crossed my mind, about Traveller, and General Lee, and that basket of raspberries? Sure beats me.

Soon as Pa realized that Lee was heading north, he commenced trying to get General Halleck to force "Fighting

Gen. George G. Meade

Joe" Hooker to follow the Rebels with the Union army, and catch up with them, and get into battle.

But "Fighting Joe" wasn't in that much of a hurry to catch Lee. He seemed to think he needed lots more soldiers and lots more time, before he could get started.

Pa sure was angry with him.

Then Hooker said maybe he should chase *south*, and try to take Richmond, while Lee was heading north.

Pa telegraphed back, not on your life! Pa said Hooker was supposed to take Lee's *army*, not the city of Richmond. And he better not let Lee take Washington or Baltimore while he was shilly-shallying.

So many telegrams in cipher was passing back and forth between Halleck and Hooker and Pa that Hooker finally got mad and said he wanted to resign his command!

Imagine that! Biggest battle of the war shaping up, and "Fighting Joe" Hooker is asking to be relieved!

Well, Pa was fit to be tied. He told General Halleck to let Hooker quit if he wanted to. So Pa and Halleck got rid of Hooker. And they put in General George Meade, in his place, on June 28.

By that time Bobby Lee's army was halfway across the state of Pennsylvania. And Pa had been calling for militia from all the nearby states. He was trying to draft soldiers into the regular army, too. But the Governor of New York state, that old fool, Horatio Seymour, said Pa didn't have the right, under the Constitution, to force citizens into the army! Not even to defend the Union!

Governor Andrew Curtin of Pennsylvania knew better

than Seymour. Right at the beginning of June he'd put up posters all over the state saying:

THE ENEMY IS APPROACHING!
I Must Rely on the People for the
DEFENSE OF THE STATE

And he called out the militia and started sending all the men he could to Harrisburg.

Well, Lee knew that General Meade was a heap better general than "Fighting Joe" Hooker. And as soon as Lee heard that Hooker was out and Meade was in, he knew he better start getting ready for a big battle.

Finally Pa was able to move up some of them blue pins on his map, because General Meade had crossed the Potomac and was moving north through Maryland, chasing General Lee.

Now Lee began pulling his army back from York and Carlisle and Chambersburg. And all his men started heading south towards Gettysburg, getting ready to have it out with Meade.

Isn't that the most confusing thing you ever heard of? The Northern army moving *north* toward Gettysburg, and the Southern army moving *south* toward Gettysburg? When you would have thought it would have been just the other way around?

The two big armies met, head on, just a bit north of Gettysburg on July 1. There's only about 1,300 people living there,

Crossing the Potomac

and it's only about eight miles north of the Mason-Dixon line between Pennsylvania and Maryland. Meade didn't have most of his men there, yet, because his army was still coming up from Maryland. And as more and more of Lee's men came piling into Gettysburg from the north, the fighting began to go against the Union troops. Finally, toward the end of the day, our Yankees had to turn and run. They ran right through the town of Gettysburg, and took up a position on some hills just south of town.

Plenty of wounded Yankee soldiers they'd had to leave behind was hid that night in cellars by the townsfolk. And Rebel troops was wandering all over the town of Gettysburg, stealing food, and tearing up barns and fence rails for firewood.

All that night, General Meade's army kept pouring up out of the South. His soldiers took up strong positions on those hills South of town. They formed a battle line in the shape of a fish hook, turned upside down, like this:

On the upper right, at the start of the curve, is Culp's Hill. Then comes Cemetery Hill. Then Cemetery Ridge, leading down to Little Round Top, and Big Round Top— two big hills at the far end of the fish hook.

Opposite Cemetery Ridge—about a mile away to the west —is another long ridge called Seminary Ridge, because there is a school, or seminary, there for Lutheran ministers

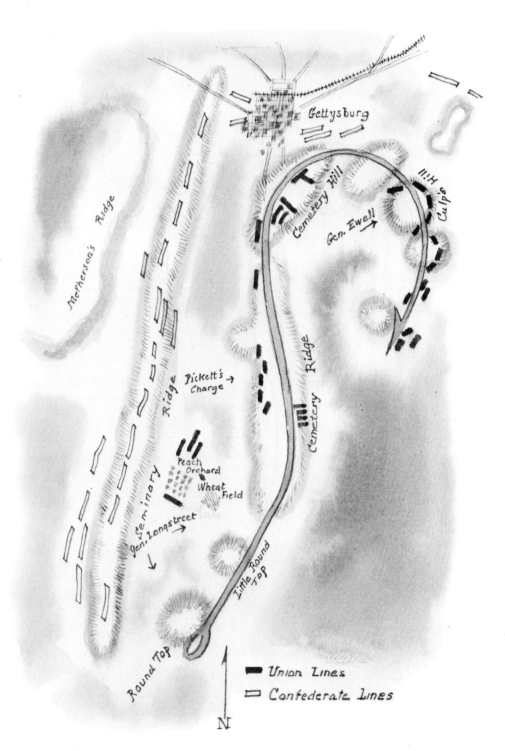

McPherson's Ridge

Gettysburg

Cemetery Hill

11th H

Gen. Ewell

Culps

Seminary Ridge

Pickett's Charge

Cemetery Ridge

Peach Orchard

Wheat Field

Gen. Longstreet

Little Round Top

Round Top

■ Union Lines

▭ Confederate Lines

N

Gen. Meade's fishhook

up on top of it. That's where most of Bobby Lee's men were posted that first night—all along that ridge.

Between the two armies there were farms—mostly wheat-fields and cornfields. And an orchard where a farmer had some peach trees set out. The fruit was almost ripe, because it was the beginning of July. All of those farmers would have cut their wheat two or three weeks earlier if they hadn't been worried with Rebels trampling all over their state.

General Meade had his headquarters in a little farmhouse on the east side of Cemetery Ridge—away from where the worst of the battle would take place. But not quite as far away as it should have been, as it turned out.

Folks said General Meade was kind of sour-tempered. Always looked like he was having an attack of acute indigestion. General Grant said he didn't want to be anywhere *near* General Meade when he was angry. And he was angry a whole lot of the time, from what I could make out. Must have been. Why else would his men have called him "the old snapping turtle"?

He knew how to fight, though. Because the next morning, on July 2, the Rebels came pounding in on both ends of his line. General Ewell's Rebels bashed at him up at Culp's Hill. And General Longstreet's Rebels bashed him in the peach orchard and the wheatfield. And in the south, at Little Round Top. But his men stood firm, and his lines held.

Late that night, General Meade sent Pa a message saying he'd repulsed the enemy at every point. Pa followed the whole thing in the telegraph office in Washington.

Pa heard that Meade held a council of war that night, on Cemetery Ridge, and decided to stay right where he was. Lee had already hit the left end and the right end of his battle line.

So Meade figured that on the next day—July 3—Lee would probably hit the center of his line, on Cemetery Ridge. Meade told his generals that's how it was going to be. But, next morning, nothing much happened at first.

"Old Snapping Turtle" Meade and a few of his officers had a lunch of stewed chicken. But before they could finish it, a huge barrage of Rebel guns opened on them, from Lee's cannon on Seminary Ridge. After three or four shells hit his headquarters, his aides were able to get old Meade to move further back, to another farmhouse, out of range of the guns.

Cannon kept firing for nearly an hour, while the earth shook, and a huge cloud of smoke blotted out the sun over the peach orchard and the wheatfield. People saw the smoke and heard the guns miles and miles away.

Pa told one of his generals—months after the battle was over—that right about this time, he locked himself in his room at the White House, and knelt down and prayed to Almighty God, asking him for victory at Gettysburg.

Then came the horrible climax of the battle. Out from Seminary Ridge came the Rebel charge—a wedge of men stretching out for a mile and a half. There was 15,000 Rebels in those lines. They was commanded by General George Pickett, of Virginia. And an officer named Armistead was

Pickett's Charge

right out in front, holding up his hat on the point of his drawn sword.

All those men were making for a little clump of oak trees on Cemetery Ridge. Right where two stone walls make an angle. Right where all of General Meade's soldiers and cannon stood waiting for them.

They came shrieking their Rebel Yell—a high quavering scream, like an Indian war whoop—over and over again.

As soon as they came in range, all of General Meade's guns went off, and screams from the wounded went up to heaven. Sometimes I have nightmares thinking about it.

The Rebel soldiers were as brave as any men could be. But they couldn't break Meade's lines. And they couldn't capture his cannon. By the time five thousand of them lay wounded or dead, they had to turn back and retreat to Seminary Ridge, where they'd come from.

That's how the most dreadful battle in the war came to an end.

They say that General Lee went out to meet them, as they staggered in off the field. He said, "This is all my fault, General Pickett. This has been my fight and the blame is mine. Your men did all men can do. The fault is entirely my own."

One of Lee's generals saw him put his head in his hands and say, "Too bad. Oh, too bad!" Because Lee knew he was defeated, and out of ammunition. He'd had thousands of his men killed, and thousands and thousands more wounded. He knew they'd have to be loaded in wagons and dragged back over bumpy roads, through the mud, to Virginia. He

Gen. George E. Pickett

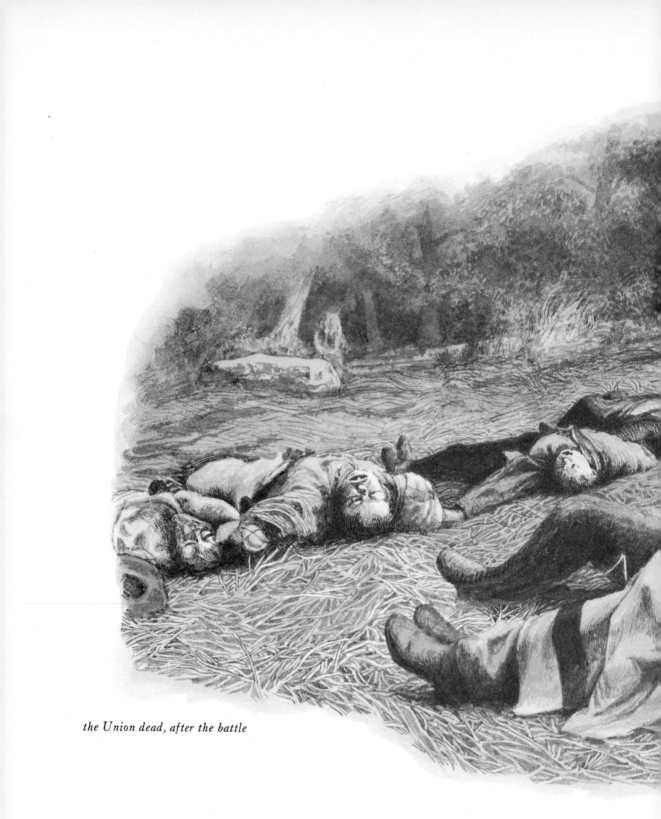

the Union dead, after the battle

must have felt just as discouraged as Pa did, when everything was going against *him*, during those first two years of the war.

Lots of times I feel terrible sorry for Pa. First of all, all these Yankee and Rebel soldiers getting killed and hurt, month after month. And no way for Pa to put a stop to it. I heard him say this war is "eating out my life," and I believe it. Another thing I heard him say, was about how he couldn't get any proper rest that would do him any real good. "Rest," said Pa, "is good for the body, I suppose. But the tired part of me is *inside* and out of reach."

I was with Pa on the Fourth of July, at the telegraph office, when he got a telegram telling him what Meade had said to the troops, that day, up in Pennsylvania. Something about how he looked to the army for even "greater efforts to drive from our soil every vestige of the presence of the invader."

Pa got mad when he heard that. He said it reminded him of another general—McClellan—who'd lost that big battle at Antietam a year earlier.

Pa said that Meade ought to be trying to ruin Lee's *army*. It wasn't enough just to save the state of Pennsylvania! "Will our generals never get that idea out of their heads?" said Pa. "The *whole country* is our soil!"

I guess Pa meant that Virginia and Georgia belong to the Union just as much as Pennsylvania does. And there isn't *any* states at all that rightfully belong to Bobby Lee and Jeffie D.

There was something else I head at the telegraph office, and I wish I hadn't. It was about all the suffering. If a soldier gets hit in the leg or the arm, most likely the bullet smashes up the bone so bad that gangrene will set in, unless the doctors amputate.

That meant there was piles and piles of arms and legs stacked up beside the hospital tents at Gettysburg after the battle. And the soldiers had nothing to deaden the pain while their arms and legs was being cut off.

It was even worse for the Rebels. Their wounded had to jounce and jostle in those horrible wagons, day after day, riding through the rain.

I heard the men in the telegraph office say that they'd heard that some of those soldiers were begging to be left behind, to die, so they wouldn't have to suffer in those wagons anymore.

"Oh, God, why can't I die?"

"My God, will no one have mercy and kill me?"

"Stop! Oh, for God's sake, stop just for one minute. Take me out and leave me to die on the roadside."

That's what we supposed those Rebels must have been saying. And it gave me terrible bad dreams to think about it.

Pa told me I could come and sleep with him, anytime I wanted to, in his big bed in the White House. That's what I been doing a lot. Especially since my brother, Willie, died last year. Because me and Willie always used to sleep together in the same room. Pa misses him just as much as I do. He said, "Since Willie's death, I catch myself talking with him as if he were with me."

Willie Lincoln

After the battle, when we went to the telegraph office, we could see the red pins pushing back toward the Potomac River, and Virginia. And the blue pins following slowly, slowly after them.

Pa was furious with General Meade for not hurrying up and catching Lee this side of the river and fighting him again. There was a chance Meade could have caught Lee's whole army. Pa actually went so far as to say that Meade *wanted* Lee to escape him.

Pa asked General Meade if he knew what he reminded him of, when his army nearly caught up with Lee on the banks of the Potomac.

"No, Mr. President. What is it?" said Meade.

"I'll be hanged if I could think of anything else," said Pa, "than an old woman trying to shoo her geese across a creek."

Anyway, Lee built himself a pontoon bridge and got clean away, across the river, on July 13. And the war keeps going on as strong as ever.

But there's one thing more about Gettysburg I've got to tell you. So many soldiers were killed up there that folks decided there should be a National Cemetery in the town, for all the fallen heroes.

They decided to dedicate the cemetery in November, four months after the big battle. Mr. David Wills—the man who suggested the whole thing—wrote Pa asking him to give a little speech at the ceremony. Pa said yes, he'd go. And Mama and I could have gone along to hear him speak—if I hadn't had to miss the whole thing because I was sick in bed with scarlatina!

Anyway, Pa left Washington for Gettysburg, by train, at around noontime, on Wednesday November 18. A whole bunch of officials went with him—Mr. Seward, his Secretary of State; Mr. Blair, his Postmaster General; and Mr. Usher, his Secretary of the Treasury. And Pa's private secretaries, Mr. Nicolay and Mr. Hay went along too. So did Pa's powerful big bodyguard, Ward Hill Lamon. Pa had his speech with him, mostly all written the week before at the telegraph office.

If I know Pa, he went up to the locomotive before he started out, to shake hands with the engineer. Pa loves to do that, because he says "I always want to see and know the man I'm riding behind."

They got to Gettysburg about six that evening, and Pa went to Mr. Will's house, on York Street, where he was going to be spending the night.

Mr. Seward was staying next door to Pa, at the Harper house. After dinner, Pa went next door, to Mr. Seward's room, to read him his speech. A big crowd collected in the street to catch a glimpse of Pa.

There was a soldier standing guard at the door of the Harper house. When Pa came out again, so many people crowded up to shake his hand he had to say to the guard, "You clear a way and I will hang onto your coat." And that's how he got back safe and sound to the Wills house!

People kept singing and hollering and serenading in the streets till all hours. Singing songs like *Tenting Tonight* and *We'll Hang Jeff Davis to a Sour Apple Tree*.

Pa put the finishing touches on his speech up in his bedroom, and then he went to sleep.

He was wearing a black suit and his tall plug hat at around ten o'clock the next morning, when the parade got started for the cemetery. He rode a good-sized bay horse, and there was bands playing and soldiers marching. Some little girl in a white dress came out to say hello to Pa, and he reached down, picked her up and sat her in front of him on his horse, and kissed her. Then he set her down, and they all moved off along Baltimore Street, heading for the cemetery.

It was a clear windy day. They'd fixed up a platform for Pa and all the rest of the main speakers and officials. Lots of governors was there, including Governor Curtin of Pennsylvania, and old Seymour from New York. Pa sat in a rocking chair, right between Mr. Seward and Mr. Edward Everett.

Mr. Everett used to be a Greek professor at Harvard, and a minister. He's said to be the very best speaker in the United States. He's been in Congress, too. Mr. Wills had asked him to give the main speech, and so he wrote and memorized a real long talk, just right for the occasion.

First there was a prayer said, then a choir from Baltimore sang a hymn, and then Mr. Everett spoke for better than an hour, about how terrible the rebellion is, and what an important battle the Battle of Gettysburg was.

Then Pa stood up. He had his speech written on two sheets of paper. But Pa's secretary Mr. Nicolay, says Pa didn't read it. He had that speech by heart. This is what he said:

Fourscore and seven years ago our fathers brought forth on this continent a new nation, conceived in liberty and dedicated to the proposition that all men are created equal. Now we are engaged in a great civil war,

the Gettysburg Address

testing whether that nation, or any nation so conceived and so dedicated, can long endure. We are met on a great battlefield of that war. We have come to dedicate a portion of that field as a final resting place for those who here gave their lives that that nation might live. It is altogether fitting and proper that we should do this. But, in a larger sense, we cannot dedicate—we cannot consecrate—we cannot hallow—this ground. The brave men, living and dead, who struggled here have consecrated it far above our poor power to add or detract. The world will little note nor long remember what we say here, but it can never forget what they did here. It is for us, the living, rather to be dedicated here to the unfinished work which they who fought here have thus far so nobly advanced. It is rather for us to be here dedicated to the great task remaining before us—that from these honored dead we take increased devotion to that cause for which they gave the last full measure of devotion; that we here highly resolve that these dead shall not have died in vain; that this nation, under God, shall have a new birth of freedom; and that government of the people, by the people, and for the people, shall not perish from the earth.

After that, Pa and Mr. Everett went off to luncheon. That afternoon, Pa asked to meet old John Burns. Mr. Burns lived in Gettysburg, where he used to be a cobbler, and for a while was constable there. At the time the battle was fought, he was way over seventy years old. But on the first of July, last summer, when he saw that the Union troops was in trouble, John

Burns grabbed his musket and fought alongside the boys in blue all that afternoon. He didn't quit until after the Rebs had wounded him three times. Everybody in town was proud of him.

Well, Pa wasn't going to miss meeting *him*! He talked for a while with the old fellow, then he walked down the street with him, arm in arm, late that afternoon. They were going to a service at the Presbyterian church. Pa and Mr. Burns prayed together in the same pew.

The next day, Mr. Everett wrote Pa a nice letter, saying Pa had said more in his two-minute speech than Mr. Everett managed to say in two hours.

I don't know about that. Because everybody says Mr. Everett's speech was grand. And not everybody seems to like what Pa had to say.

But I can say *this* for Pa. He thinks and talks a lot straighter than Jeffie D. and Bobby Lee. At Gettysburg, *they* claimed to be after a little clump of oak trees on Cemetery Ridge, so that their "beloved country" could be independent, and could go on owning slaves.

Well, Pa believes that *this* country belongs to *all* of us—not just to the ones of us who's white. And when all those boys died at Gettysburg, that's what they was dying for—so's *all* men could be free and equal, like we claim they was created.

At least, that's what I take Pa to mean. Why else would he say "a *new* birth of freedom"?

the Devil's Den, at Gettysburg

About this story

This story is fiction, for it is told as if Tad Lincoln (1853–1871) were recounting all the events and circumstances of the Battle of Gettysburg (July 1, 2, 3, 1863) as well as the events of the dedication of the National Cemetery there on November 19 of the same year.

Tad was Abraham Lincoln's favorite son, and he had constant access to his father—interrupting his sleep in the middle of the night, and his cabinet meetings by day. Nevertheless, only in fiction could Tad have experienced and related everything attributed to him here —though everything set forth is based on fact.

The grisly horrors of Gettysburg, in which over 5,000 men died (Confederate losses in killed and wounded were 20,451; while Union losses were 23,003) have not been emphasized. Instead, I have tried to let Lincoln himself summarize the meaning of Gettysburg. His own words cannot be surpassed, for, as Carl Sandburg has written of the Gettysburg Address, Lincoln's "outwardly smooth sentences were inside of them gnarled and tough with the enigmas of the American experiment."

Bibliography

The Education of Henry Adams, by Henry Adams. Random House, New York, 1918.

The Lincoln Reader, ed. by Paul M. Angle. Pocket Books, New York, 1947.

Lincoln in the Telegraph Office, by David Homer Bates. The Century Co., New York, 1907.

Gettysburg and Lincoln, by Henry Sweetser Burrage. Putnam's, New York, 1906.

Lincoln's Gettysburg Address, by Orton H. Carmichael. Abingdon, New York, 1971.

The Battle of Gettysburg, by Bruce Catton. American Heritage Publishing Co., New York, 1963.

The Civil War, by Bruce Catton. American Heritage Publishing Co., New York, 1960.

Abraham Lincoln, by Lord Charnwood (Godfrey Rathone Benson). Pocket Books, New York, 1939.

R. E. Lee: A Biography, by Douglas Southall Freeman. Scribner's, New York, 1935.

Edward Everett: Orator and Statesman, by Paul Revere Frothingham. Houghton, Mifflin, Boston, 1925.

Twenty Days, by Dorothy Meserve Kunhardt and Philip B. Kunhardt, Jr. Harper, New York, 1965.

Lincoln: A Picture Story of His Life, by Stefan Lorant. Harper, New York, 1957.

Abraham Lincoln: A History, by John G. Nicolay and Hay. The Century Co., New York, 1890.

Turnpikes and Dirt Roads (containing the story of David Clough meeting Robert E. Lee), by Leighton Parks. Scribner's, New York, 1927.

Abraham Lincoln (The Prairie Years and The War Years, one volume ed.), by Carl Sandburg. Harcourt, Brace, New York, 1954.

They Met at Gettysburg, by Edward J. Stackpole. Eagle Books, Harrisburgh, Pa., 1956.

Embattled Confederates, by Bell Irvin Wiley. Harper, New York, 1964.

Lincoln and His Generals, by T. Harry Williams. Knopf, New York, 1963.